I
Loathe
You

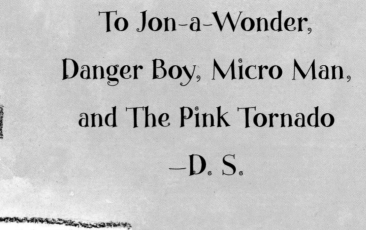

To Jon-a-Wonder,
Danger Boy, Micro Man,
and The Pink Tornado
—D. S.

 ALADDIN

An imprint of Simon & Schuster Children's Publishing Division

1230 Avenue of the Americas, New York, NY 10020

First Aladdin hardcover edition December 2012

Copyright © 2012 by David Slonim

For information about special discounts for bulk purchases, please contact Simon & Schuster Special Sales
at 1-866-506-1949 or business@simonandschuster.com.

The Simon & Schuster Speakers Bureau can bring authors to your live event. For more information
or to book an event contact the Simon & Schuster Speakers Bureau at 1-866-248-3049 or visit our website
at www.simonspeakers.com.

Designed by Lisa Vega

The text of this book was set in Fiddlestix.

The illustrations for this book were rendered in acrylic with charcoal.

Manufactured in China 0912 SCP

10 9 8 7 6 5 4 3 2 1

This book has been cataloged with the Library of Congress.

ISBN 978-1-4424-2244-5

ISBN 978-1-4424-5709-6 (eBook)

I Loathe You

Written and Illustrated by David Slonim

ALADDIN

New York   London   Toronto   Sydney   New Delhi

Little Monster said,
"I loathe you."

Big Monster said,
"I loathe you, too."

"How much?"
said the small one sheepishly.

Big monster smiled and said,
"Let's see . . ."

....That Causes Fits
All The News
The Daily Scare
A BUMP IN THE NIGHT
Squeaky Door Not An Open And Shut Case

"I loathe you more than chicken pox,
more than stinky, sweaty socks.

More than garbage in a dump,

or splinters
sticking in
my rump.

Mosquito bites?
I loathe them, yes,
But next to you,
a whole lot less."

Little Monster scratched its head
then crinkled up its nose and said,

"I loathe YOU more
than bellyaches!"

Big Monster grinned.
"For goodness' sakes!

"I loathe you more than slimy rats,
more than frostbite, skunks, or bats!

More than fuzzy mold on cheese,
    more than fever or disease!

Picture lobsters pinching me. . . .
    I loathe you more—now do you see?"

Little Monster shook its head,
   then twisting up its tail it said,

"If you were sunburned,
   red and sore,
Would you loathe
   ME even more?"

Big Monster grinned from horn to horn.
"I dreamed of you before you were born!

Think how deep my loathing reaches—
more than ticks or slimy leeches.

More than what the cat dragged in,
with what the dog threw up thrown in!"

Little Monster turned slightly red,
then in a little voice it said,

"But what if I goof up someday,
or if my warts all fade away?

If I blurt out 'THANKS,' or 'PLEASE'?
Or take a bath and kill my fleas?

If I should slip and just obey
then would your loathing go away?"

"What if I stop chewing chairs,

or

bouncing

goldfish

down

the

stairs?"

"Suppose someday
I lose my stink?
What would
you say?
What would
you think?"

Big Monster smiled and shook its head.
"Did you not hear what I just said?"

Nice or nasty, kind or mean,
  I loathe you up, down, and between.

From your horns down to your claws,
  you're mine! I loathe you just because—

Snout to tail, scales and fuzz,
  always will be, always was."

"Now shut your peepers
and your snoot,
And go to sleep,
my little brute!"